WHY RAT COMES FIRST

A Story of the Chinese Zodiac

Retold by Clara Yen
Illustrated by Hideo C. Yoshida

CHILDREN'S BOOK PRESS
San Francisco, California

In heaven, high above the milk-white clouds, the Jade King sat and watched over China.

Funny and sad stories about China's animals often reached his ears, but he had never set eyes upon them.

Being curious, he decided to invite these creatures to a great feast so he could finally meet them.

The Jade King sent the prime minister down to earth with his arms full of red invitations for the animal guests. The prime minister was used to walking on soft, fluffy clouds, but not on hard, rocky ground. He tripped on a stone, fell to the dirt, and dropped his invitations. As he crawled about to gather them together, a gust of wind lifted them up and sent them soaring away. Sadly, the prime minister returned to heaven.

"It doesn't matter," consoled the Jade King. "Whoever receives my invitations shall be welcomed through our door. Perhaps it is better that the wind does the traveling and saves you the trouble."

The invitations read: "Calling upon China's wondrous beasts. You are invited to dine at the Jade King's Feast."

After the coldest winter nights had passed and before the warmest spring days had arrived, the food was cooked, the lanterns were hung, and the great feast was ready.

"Imagine," thought the Jade King, "I am finally going to meet the thousands of animals that soar through the sky, walk on the land, and swim through the sea." Then the Jade King sat down to wait.

M y King!" announced the prime minister. "Your guests have arrived!" And he opened the doors to let the animals in. The Jade King counted the animals, then the corners of his smile turned down. Though thousands of animals roamed the earth, only twelve had entered heaven's gate.

Although he felt sad that so few animals came, the Jade King did not want to spoil the celebration. So he turned to the animals and said, "By coming today, you twelve have properly paid your respects to me and I wish to reward you. There are twelve years in our calendar cycle and there are twelve animals at our great feast. Twelve animals, twelve years. I hereby name one year after each animal that is here today."

The animals said, "We thank you, Jade King, for inviting us here. We are honored to give our names to a year."

Excuse me, my great king," said Rat, "but which animal comes first? I am clever and very smart. The year should have me at the start."

"Excuse me, king of one thousand years," said Ox, "but I am mighty and very strong. Starting with me could not be wrong."

"Clever and smart, mighty and strong?" thought the Jade King. He turned to the other animals. "Which one should come first?"

The animals began to argue.

"Clever Rat uses his brain.
When Ox tries to think, it gives him a pain."

"Hard-working Ox stands proud and tall.
Lowly Rat is much too small."

C lose your mouths!" commanded the Jade King. He paced around the room, stroking his beard. "Since you animals cannot decide, I shall hold a contest, a popularity contest, between Rat and Ox. The judges will be the children on earth. The winner will be the animal that the children decide is . . . ." He paused to think. "The most special," he finally announced.

The animals nodded their heads in agreement.

The Jade King told his prime minister to take Rat and Ox down to earth, to a village courtyard where children were playing.

Ox trotted up to the children and strolled comfortably around them. While working on his master's farm, he had often let the children ride on his back and they were used to his big, brown body. Even the smallest child was not afraid to ride the strong but gentle beast.

Rat began to complain. "Ox is too big and I'm too small. He is easily seen by all. Make me bigger so the contest is fair. Make me as big as Ox out there."

The prime minister considered Rat's request. Then he nodded his head and clapped his hands. Rat grew and grew until he was as big as a hundred rats. Delighted, he ran into the courtyard to join Ox.

The children jumped
up and down and
waved their arms.

"Ooohh, such a huge rat!"

"Aaiiiyaaa!
Look, look, look!
It's a great big rat!"

The children forgot all about Ox.

A few minutes later the prime minister walked into the courtyard and told the children, "The Jade King is having a contest. He wants to know which animal you think is the most special —Rat or Ox?"

"The rat! The rat! I've never seen a rat as big as that!"

"It's true! It's true! I saw it, too!"

"Did you see? Did you see? That rat was big, as big as me!"

The prime minister wrote down the children's words. Then he returned to heaven with Rat and Ox and reported the day's events to the Jade King.

According to your report," said the Jade King, "the children have chosen Rat—although he was somewhat big." The Jade King smiled to himself. "I hereby proclaim that Rat is the winner. Rat, you will lead the first year. Furthermore, all children born this year and every year of the Rat will be as clever as you were today."

"Let us now celebrate!"

The Jade King took the animals, led by Rat, into the decorated banquet hall. Surrounded by plates of delicious food,

the animals raised their cups and wished
each other and the Jade King good health,
long life, and happiness.

A NOTE FROM THE AUTHOR

According to the Chinese lunar calendar, the new year begins on the second new moon after the first day of winter. This day usually falls in late January or February. Each year is named after a different animal. Children born during that year are believed to have characteristics of the animal. Twelve years form one zodiac cycle.

Find the year in which you were born to see what animal sign you are.

RAT Honest, ambitious, and clever

1900 1912 1924 1936 1948 1960 1972 1984 1996 2008
You get along with Dragon and Monkey, but not with Horse.

OX Bright, patient, and hard-working

1901 1913 1925 1937 1949 1961 1973 1985 1997 2009
You get along with Snake and Rooster, but not with Sheep.

TIGER Courageous, powerful, and adventuresome

1902 1914 1926 1938 1950 1962 1974 1986 1998 2010
You get along with Horse and Dog, but not with Monkey.

HARE Caring, talented, and graceful

1903 1915 1927 1939 1951 1963 1975 1987 1999 2011
You get along with Sheep and Boar, but not with Rooster.

DRAGON Energetic, healthy, and powerful

1904 1916 1928 1940 1952 1964 1976 1988 2000 2012
You get along with Monkey and Rat, but not with Dog.

SNAKE Wise, calm, and elegant

1905 1917 1929 1941 1953 1965 1977 1989 2001 2013
You get along with Rooster and Ox, but not with Boar.

HORSE Attractive, independent, and stylish

1906 1918 1930 1942 1954 1966 1978 1990 2002 2014
You get along with Tiger and Dog, but not with Rat.

SHEEP Gentle, artistic, and creative

1907 1919 1931 1943 1955 1967 1979 1991 2003 2015
You get along with Boar and Hare, but not with Ox.

MONKEY Intelligent, organized, enthusiastic

1908 1920 1932 1944 1956 1968 1980 1992 2004 2016
You get along with Dragon and Rat, but not with Tiger.

ROOSTER Careful, independent, and hard-working

1909 1921 1933 1945 1957 1969 1981 1993 2005 2017
You get along with Snake and Ox, but not with Hare.

DOG Honest, loyal, and generous

1910 1922 1934 1946 1958 1970 1982 1994 2006 2018
You get along with Horse and Tiger, but not with Dragon.

BOAR Generous, helpful, and noble

1911 1923 1935 1947 1959 1971 1983 1995 2007 2019
You get along with Hare and Sheep, but not with other Boars.

ABOUT THE STORY

In books of folk and fairy tales, you can find many stories about how the twelve animals of the Chinese zodiac were chosen, why they appear in their order, and why Rat comes first. My father read many of these stories to me. But the story we liked best was the one he made up, which I adapted for this book. I would like to dedicate *Why Rat Comes First* to my father, Charles Chia Shiang Yen, and my mother, Florence Kwang Tsung Yen.

Clara Yen

Clara Yen, a second generation Chinese American, is an elementary school teacher and professional storyteller. She says she heard her first story when her father told her what happens to little girls who don't brush their teeth. Since then she has been collecting and sharing family, folk, and fairy tales with San Francisco Bay Area audiences.

Hideo C. Yoshida, a third generation Japanese American, is an artist, printmaker and theatrical designer whose work is shown throughout the San Francisco Bay Area. He has created sets and costumes for the Asian American Theater Company and has worked with children to build floats for the Chinese New Year parade. His silkscreen posters, including a series on the animals of the Chinese zodiac, are now collector's items. He used ink and colored pencil for *Why Rat Comes First*, his first book for Children's Book Press.

Editors: Harriet Rohmer and David Schecter   Design: Nancy Hom   Production: Alex Torres and Tony Yuen
Printed in China through Marwin Productions. Children's Book Press is a nonprofit community publisher.

Library of Congress Cataloging-in-Publication Data
Yen, Clara. Why rat comes first; a story of the Chinese zodiac / retold by
Clara Yen; illustrated by Hideo C. Yoshida.   p.cm.
Summary: Explains why Rat comes first in the Chinese calendar cycle of twelve years.
ISBN   0-89239-072-7   [1. Astrology. Chinese--Fiction.] I. Yoshida, Hideo C., ill. II. Title.
Pz7.Y379Wh   1991   [Fic]--dc20   90-26536 CIP AC